D0408778

# HORSEBACK
## Hurdles

## BY JAKE MADDOX

text by Emma Carlson Berne

illustrations by Katie Wood

STONE ARCH BOOKS
a capstone imprint

Jake Maddox books are published by Stone Arch Books
A Capstone Imprint
1710 Roe Crest Drive
North Mankato, Minnesota 56003
www.capstonepub.com

Library of Congress Cataloging-in-Publication Data
Maddox, Jake.
Horseback hurdles / by Jake Maddox ; text by Emma Carlson Berne ; illustrated
by Katie Wood.
p. cm. -- (Jake Maddox sports story)
Summary: Mia has been volunteering with her best friend Sky at the Rocky
Ridge Riding Center for three months, but she keeps getting in trouble because
of her lack of focus--can working with the troubled horse, Diamond, help her to
save both of them for the Riding Center?
ISBN 978-1-4342-3294-6 (library binding)
ISBN 978-1-4342-3905-1 (pbk.)
1. Horses--Juvenile fiction. 2. Riding schools--Juvenile fiction. 3. Human-
animal relationships--Juvenile fiction. 4. Self-confidence--Juvenile fiction. 5.
Best friends--Juvenile fiction. [1. Horses--Fiction. 2. Horsemanship--Fiction. 3.
Riding schools--Fiction.] I. Berne, Emma Carlson. II. Wood, Katie, ill. III. Title.
IV. Series.

PZ7.M25643HP 2012
813.6--DC23

2011032222

Designer: Heather Kindseth
Production Specialist: Michelle Biedscheid

Printed in the United States of America in Stevens Point, Wisconsin.
102011
006404WZS12

# TABLE OF CONTENTS

## Chapter One

# MIA'S MISTAKE

Mia was sweeping the stable floor. She heard the head instructor, Maren, shouting.

"Girls!" Maren called. "Everyone out here! The pasture gate was left open again. Trixie and Diamond are out!"

Mia dropped the broom. It clattered to the floor.

Her stomach sank. She had been the last one out to the pasture.

*Oh no! Not again!* thought Mia. *I was the last one out. Did I lock the gate?*

Mia had been volunteering at the Rocky Ridge Riding Center for three months. So far, she'd left the pasture gate open twice. It was pretty much the worst mistake you could make.

"Mia, come on!" her best friend, Sky, yelled. "What are you waiting for?"

"Nothing," Mia said. She hurried toward Sky.

"Wait, Mia!" Sky exclaimed. "Aren't you going to pick up the broom? Maren says we're not supposed to leave tools on the barn floor."

"Oh, right," Mia mumbled. She picked up the broom and propped it against the wall.

Mia was always doing stuff like that. She needed to focus more. She also needed to be more careful.

Mia and Sky grabbed halters and lead ropes.

"I'll go close the gate to the road," Maren called. "You two catch the horses."

"Got it," Mia replied. Trixie and Diamond were standing in a grassy area. Beside them, the pasture gate was wide open.

Diamond's coat gleamed in the sunlight. He had arrived at the stable only three months ago, like Mia. Diamond was Mia's favorite.

But Diamond wasn't perfect. In fact, he had some serious problems. He had been biting students and other horses.

"I'll see if I can catch Diamond," Mia said to Sky. "You catch Trixie."

Sky's forehead wrinkled. "Trixie is easy to get. But are you sure you can catch Diamond?" she asked. "He tried to bite me last week."

Mia rolled her eyes. "Of course I can catch him," she said.

Sky shrugged. She went over to Trixie. The mare stood calmly while Sky slipped a halter on her.

Now it was Mia's turn. She walked up to Diamond. She held the halter behind her back. He was watching her. Mia knew it was going to be tricky.

"Hi, boy," Mia said. "I know you're having fun, but it's time to go in."

She whipped her hand out fast. She tried to slide the halter on. But her hand accidently knocked Diamond above the eye. He flattened his ears and snapped at her hand.

Mia gasped. She snatched her hand away. She'd been too fast and had scared the horse.

Then Maren's hand fell on Mia's shoulder. "Mia, you're being too quick with that horse," her instructor said.

She took the halter from Mia's hand. Slowly, the instructor slid it over the horse's head.

"Horses don't like hands flying around," Maren said.

"Sorry," Mia muttered. "I was just trying to help."

"Sky, please put Trixie in her stall," Maren went on. "And Mia, I'd like to see you in my office."

Maren began leading Diamond toward the stable.

Mia and Sky stared at each other. Mia swallowed. Whatever Maren wanted to discuss, it wasn't going to be good.

## Chapter Two

# MAREN'S DECISION

Maren was sitting behind her desk in the stable office when Mia arrived at the door. Her heart was pounding.

"Come in, Mia," Maren said. Her face was serious.

"I'm sorry, Maren," she blurted. "I know I've messed up before but —"

"Please sit down, Mia," Maren said.

"Okay," Mia said.

"You were the last one scheduled to take Trixie and Diamond out to the pasture," Maren said. "Were you the last one out of the gate?"

"I think so," Mia answered.

"This is the third time you've left the gate open," Maren said. "I've told you before that this is dangerous."

Mia stared at her feet.

Maren flipped through some papers. "I've just been reading over your volunteer record," she said. "Mia, you have a history of making careless mistakes. You act before you think." Maren sighed. "I know you care about the horses. But we can't have these kinds of problems. You cannot volunteer here anymore. You'll have to gather your belongings and call your mother."

"I-I'm sorry," Mia said, sniffling. "I never meant to leave the gate open so many times."

Maren put an arm around Mia. "I know you didn't mean it, Mia," she said. "But it's just too risky to keep you here."

Mia went outside to call her mom. She would have to explain what happened. And then her mom would scold her for being careless again.

"Well, this horse will have to be sold," a voice said nearby.

Mia looked around. Two of the younger instructors, Ben and Sara, were standing next to Diamond. They did not see Mia.

Mia leaned in to hear exactly what they were saying.

"I agree," Sara said. "Watch this." She reached up to pat Diamond's neck. But the horse quickly laid his ears back and turned to bite.

"Diamond, stop!" Ben said sternly. "He's too dangerous to be kept here. We don't want him hurting a student or another horse."

Sara sighed. "We'd better tell Maren."

Diamond stood quietly. His proud neck was arched. *He doesn't know he's about to be sold,* Mia thought. *He's just like me. Both of us are being sent away.*

Mia put her hand on the phone to call her mother. Suddenly, she stopped. An amazing plan had just flashed through her head. It was crazy. But if it worked, it just might save both her and Diamond.

Chapter Three

# THE CRAZY PLAN

Mia hurried back into the barn. She ran into Maren's office.

"Maren? Can I talk to you?" she asked.

Her instructor looked up. "What is it, Mia?" she asked.

"I have an idea," Mia said. "I know you might not like it. But I wanted to ask anyway." Her voice shook. "I heard that Diamond is going to be sold."

"Yes, that's right," Maren said. She nodded. "He isn't working out. He's just too dangerous."

"What if I could have one more chance here? And Diamond could too?" Mia asked. "I could work with Diamond every day."

"I don't know," Maren said.

"It would be a kind of test for me," Mia said. "I want to show you that I can work here without making any careless mistakes. I know that we both can get better."

Maren tapped her finger against her cheek. Then she nodded. "All right, Mia. I'll give you and Diamond one more chance," Maren said.

"Oh, thank you!" Mia exclaimed. "You won't regret this, really!"

"But there's one more thing," Maren said. "You both must show that you've improved by the time of the Rocky Ridge Rumpus. That means no biting for Diamond. And no careless mistakes for you."

The Rocky Ridge Rumpus was the student horse show at the barn. It was only four days away! Could she really get Diamond to improve by then?

But this was her only chance. "It's a deal," Mia said, sticking out her hand.

"Done," Maren replied.

They shook hands.

"Good luck, Mia," Maren said. "I'll be rooting for you!"

Chapter Four

# REMEMBER YOUR MISTAKES

That night after dinner, Mia flopped across her bed. She called Sky.

"Hi!" Mia squealed when her best friend answered. "Guess what happened?"

Quickly, Mia explained her crazy plan. "Well?" she said when she was finished. "Isn't that awesome?

"I guess," Sky answered.

"Diamond is going to be the best horse in the stable when I'm done," Mia said.

"I don't know," Sky replied slowly. "Diamond's really hard to handle. And how are you going to stop making all those mistakes?"

"I haven't made that many mistakes," Mia replied.

"Remember when you left that whole bag of grain out?" Sky said. "The mice got in it. Or how about when you left those saddles outside all night and it rained? Or how about when —"

"Okay, I get it!" Mia said. She sat up on her bed. "I thought you'd be happy."

"I am," Sky insisted. "I just don't want you to get into something you can't handle."

"I can handle it," Mia said.

"Fine," Sky replied.

"Fine," Mia said.

They were both silent.

"Well, I guess I'll see you at the barn tomorrow," Sky finally said.

"Yeah, see you," Mia replied. She hung up the phone and sat on her bed, staring out the window. Sky's words repeated in her head. Maybe her friend was right. Was this whole plan just another big mistake?

Chapter Five

# THE DIAMOND DILEMMA

It was only seven o'clock when Mia slid into Diamond's stall the next morning. Mia wanted to get started on her project as soon as possible. The show was only three days away.

Today, her plan was to get to know Diamond better. She needed to figure out why he was always trying to bite. Then tomorrow, she'd ride him in her regular riding lesson.

The barn was chilly this early. It was also very quiet. Diamond was standing with his head near the stall door. He was finishing the last of his breakfast.

"Hey, boy," Mia said, sliding the door back with a bang. Right away, Diamond flicked his ears back and rolled his eyes. He let out a warning nicker.

Mia gasped. She backed out of the stall fast. She slid the door shut and leaned against it. She was breathing fast.

This was going to be a little harder than she'd thought. But it was her only chance. It was his only chance, too.

After a second, she slowly slid back the door and peeked inside. Diamond gave her a suspicious look. Mia eyed him back, then took a deep breath.

"Hi, Diamond," she said in a low, calm voice.

The horse's ears flickered, but he didn't pin them back.

Mia slowly slid the stall door closed behind her. Slow and steady, that's what she needed to be. She walked forward as carefully as she could. She gently patted Diamond's shoulder.

"There, boy," she said. "That's not too bad, right?"

Diamond relaxed a little. He lowered his head. He blew some air out of his nose. Then he poked his muzzle in the direction of her pocket.

"Oh, is this what you're looking for?" Mia asked. She thrust her hand in her pocket and pulled out an apple.

But she moved too fast. The apple snagged on her pocket. She tugged it loose, and her hand flew up. She smacked Diamond right on the nose!

He jerked his head up, shaking it a little. He rolled his eyes in surprise. His whole body was tense. Mia could see that if she made one wrong move, he'd try to bite her.

She backed away against the wall of the stall. Okay, that was an error. She'd moved too fast and scared him. She wasn't going to do that again.

Mia watched Diamond until he calmed down. Then she reached into the tack box that sat just outside the door.

She pulled out a soft brush. Maybe a little grooming would help him relax.

Diamond stood quietly as she ran the brush over his shoulders and along his back. Mia finished brushing his neck. He stood quietly. Then Mia raised her hand to brush his ears.

As soon as she touched his ears with the brush, Diamond jerked his head up. He backed away from her. His muscles tensed up. He started shaking.

Mia gasped and pulled her hand away. She knocked her elbow against the metal hayrack, making a loud clanging noise. Diamond let out a warning nicker. He began pacing in the stall. He was nervous and upset.

Mia held out her hand. Diamond rolled his eyes at her. He pinned his ears back.

Mia's heart sank. She had made so much progress. Now it seemed like they were back where they started.

At least she knew what Diamond's problem was. He didn't like anyone touching his head.

Like yesterday, when she'd tried to put his halter on too fast. And earlier, when she banged the stall door near his head. He might have been treated roughly at his last home. Or maybe he'd always had this fear.

"Is that it, boy?" Mia asked Diamond. "You get nervous when people touch your head?"

As she spoke, she moved toward him very slowly. Mia firmly patted him on the neck.

Diamond didn't move. Mia worked her way over his back. She talked to Diamond all the time. He stood quietly with his head down. Mia didn't try to touch his head again.

After several minutes, Mia slowly backed out of the stall. She wasn't used to moving this carefully. But she knew she couldn't make any more mistakes. She latched the door and double-checked it.

*Only two more days left,* Mia thought. And her lesson was tomorrow. How was she going to put a bridle on him if she couldn't touch his ears?

Chapter Six

# MAREN STEPS IN

The next afternoon, Mia found Sky in Trixie's stall.

"Sky!" she called, panting up to her friend. "I need some help."

"What?" Sky asked. She wiped her arm across her forehead. "Did Diamond bite you yet?"

"Not yet," Mia told her. "I think he's starting to trust me."

"So what's the problem?" Sky asked.

"He won't let me touch his ears," Mia said. "Now I can't bridle him! And I'm supposed to have my lesson in fifteen minutes."

"Oh boy," Sky agreed. "Maren hates it when people are late for lessons."

"I know!" Mia said. "Any ideas?"

"I'll come help you," Sky said. "Trixie will be fine for a second."

The two friends walked fast to Diamond's stall. They didn't have much time.

"I got his saddle on without any trouble," Mia said. "He doesn't mind if you just move really slowly. Be really, really careful."

"Slowly? Be careful? I've never heard you talk like that before. Or move like that!" Sky said, smiling.

Mia shrugged. She slid back the bolt on Diamond's door. Sky stepped up beside the horse.

"What do you want me to do?" she asked.

"Can you stand on the other side of his head?" Mia asked. "I'll get the bridle around his ears. You take one side. I'll take the other. We'll just slide it right over."

"That doesn't sound too bad," Sky said. She stepped over to Diamond's right.

*Slow and careful*, Mia told herself. She draped the reins over Diamond's neck, just like Maren had taught her.

The horse stood quietly. His head was tense. So far, so good.

Mia pressed her thumb into the corner of Diamond's lips. He opened his teeth. She slid the bit over his molars and into the back of his mouth. Now for the ears.

Mia realized she'd been holding her breath. She forced herself to exhale. At the same time, she lifted the headstall up. Sky reached over.

But just as Mia touched the tips of his ears, Diamond reared his head. His neck quivered. His eyes rolled.

"Shoot!" Mia muttered. She lowered her hand and looked at Sky.

"I see your problem," her friend said, her eyes wide.

"Yeah," Mia replied, sighing.

"Try again," Sky urged.

Once again, Mia raised the headstall and tried to slip it into place. This time, she actually got it most of the way over one ear. Almost there!

She tried to jam the other ear into place. But Diamond felt the rough touch. He let out a warning whinny. He quickly backed away into the corner.

Mia felt all the progress she'd made slipping through her fingers.

"My lesson's in two minutes!" she wailed, the bridle dangling from her fingers.

Just then, Maren appeared at the stall door. "And you know how I like students to be on time," she chimed in.

Maren opened the stall door. She took the bridle from Mia's hand. She slid it smoothly over Diamond's head. She buckled a few straps. He was finally wearing a bridle.

"Sometimes horses will only let people they trust touch their ears," Maren said. "Looks like you two still have a little ways to go."

She went out the stall door. Mia looked at Sky and swallowed.

"Time for my lesson," Mia said in a brave voice.

"Good luck," Sky said.

Sky squeezed her friend's shoulder. Mia nodded back. She had a feeling she was going to need all the luck she could get.

Chapter 7

# NO MISTAKES

Mia climbed onto Diamond's back. She took a deep breath. It was time to tackle Diamond's problems in the ring. He didn't like other horses getting too close to him. He would bite them if they did. That could injure both the horse and the rider.

They rode out to the ring. Mia reminded herself that she couldn't make any mistakes. Diamond could not be allowed to get too close to other horses.

That meant that Mia had to stay alert. She had to be careful the entire time.

*You can do it,* Mia told herself. *Stay focused, stay calm.*

Mia controlled her breathing. Her body steadied. She felt her hands steady, too. Diamond relaxed. He lowered his head and chewed the bit.

Mia and Diamond entered the ring. Sky smiled at them. She was riding Trixie. Mia grinned back. But she took her eyes off the scene in front of her. She almost walked Diamond into Bobby, a big bay horse.

Quickly, Mia turned before they could get too close. Shoot! One mistake, right at the start. This wasn't looking good for her and Diamond.

"All right, everyone!" Maren called. "Let's start with a nice walk around the ring."

She eyed the riders. After a moment, she called, "Okay, very nice. Let's have a posting trot!"

Gently, Mia squeezed Diamond into a trot. She watched the horse in front of them. When they got a little close, she swung Diamond off the rail. They trotted across the ring to a big open space.

"Very good, Mia!" she heard Maren call. "Nice watching."

Mia's face flushed with pleasure. She warned herself not to get too confident.

Just then, Bobby trotted right up behind Diamond. His rider, Erin, was staring out at the trees.

Mia felt Diamond's body tense. She saw his ears flatten. Any second now, he was going to try to bite Bobby. That would be the end of them both.

Mia thought fast. She turned Diamond out into the middle. She looked for an open spot on the rail. Her heart was hammering. If she hadn't seen Bobby, Diamond would have bitten him.

*I never would have noticed that before,* Mia thought.

Maren propped two white poles in a low X in the center of the ring.

"All right, everyone," she called out. "We've been practicing jumping position for a few weeks now. Let's try it over a crossrail."

Sky and Mia exchanged excited glances. Ever since they started riding, they'd been dreaming of jumping.

The riders lined up. One by one, they trotted their horses carefully down the center of the ring and over the crossrail.

Erin's horse refused to trot over the rail. He stepped over it instead. Trixie went around it, even though Sky was directing her straight ahead.

When it was Mia's turn, she pressed her heels gently into Diamond's sides. She was careful to keep her hands low and still as he trotted.

Mia rose out of the saddle. She leaned forward. She pressed her heels down and kept her eyes up.

Then Diamond made a little leap. They were over!

"Very nice, Mia!" Maren called. "Pull up near the gate, please, everyone."

The riders clustered around their instructor. "As you all know, the Rocky Ridge Rumpus is tomorrow," Maren said. "You all may register for your class on the clipboard outside my office. Nice job today!"

"Are you going to do the crossrail class, Mia?" Sky asked.

"Do you think I should?" Mia said.

Sky nodded. "Yeah," she said. "Mia and Diamond take Rocky Ridge Riding Center by storm!"

Mia laughed. For the first time, she let herself believe that her crazy plan was going to work out.

## Chapter 8

# TRUST

"Mia, are you sure you want me to leave you so early?" Mom said the morning of the show. "There's nobody else here."

Mia nodded. "I'm sure, Mom," she said. "I need some extra time with Diamond."

"All right," Mom said. "Dad and I will be back later. We'll be watching for you!"

Mia waved as Mom drove away. But as soon as the minivan was out of sight, she frowned.

Diamond still wouldn't let her bridle him. It was so frustrating! She'd been so careful. She hadn't made one careless mistake. And he'd made so much progress.

But she couldn't ride him in the show if she couldn't get his bridle on. And something told her that Maren wouldn't be around to rescue her today.

Diamond pricked his ears as she slid back his stall door. He nuzzled her pocket for his treat. She quietly patted his neck.

"Big day today, boy," she told him.

He crunched his carrot noisily. Little bits of orange fell from his lips.

"I need some help, okay?" she said to him. "I need you to trust me." She looked into his huge brown eyes. He gazed back calmly.

Mia grabbed the grooming box. She curried Diamond's coat until it gleamed. Then she combed out his long mane and tail. She lifted the saddle into place and buckled the girth.

She could hear other riders arriving. They were loudly talking to each other. Stall doors clanged everywhere.

Sky's face appeared at Diamond's stall door. "Hey!" she said. "Trixie rolled in the pasture. She's got dried mud all over her. How's Diamond?"

"Great," said Mia. "He hasn't tried to bite once. But then again, I haven't tried *that* yet either." She nodded toward the bridle hanging outside the stall door.

"Remember what Maren said. He just has to trust you," Sky reminded her.

"I know," Mia said.

"Got to go. I have to start washing Trixie. See you in the ring," Sky said as she waved goodbye.

Mia took a deep breath. She lifted the bridle off the hook. Diamond eyed the bridle suspiciously.

"Just you and me now, boy," she muttered.

Mia draped the reins over Diamond's neck. She steeled herself. Then, carefully and slowly, she fit the bit into his mouth. She brought her hand up over his forehead. This was the hard part.

Diamond didn't move. He stood, tense. Mia sensed he was about to try to jerk away. But instead of getting tense in return, she forced her body to relax.

Her hands were soft and steady. She murmured, "There now, there now," over and over.

Mia felt the muscles in Diamond's neck relax. Then he actually lowered his head a few inches. This was it! Mia knew she'd only get one chance. If she didn't get the bridle on the first time, she wasn't going to get it on at all.

Mia put her hand on Diamond's long, velvety ears. He held still. She could feel his breath whooshing in and out. It was hot on her arm. She slid the bit into his mouth. No problem there.

She slowly reached her hand gently up his face toward his ears. She slid the headstall into place over one ear. She expected him to jerk away. But Diamond didn't move.

Now the other ear. There it was! She did it! Mia smoothed his forelock. She buckled the throatlatch. She stood back, breathing hard. She did it!

Diamond looked back at her as if he didn't believe what had just happened. Three days ago, Mia would have hugged him around the neck. But now she just patted him calmly.

"Good boy!" she said in a low, happy voice.

Just then she heard Maren call, "Okay, riders, let's go!"

Mia buckled on her helmet. She took hold of Diamond's reins. It was showtime.

*Chapter 9*

# THE ROCKY RIDGE RUMPUS

Mia rode into the ring. The bleachers where full. Banners draped on the rails of the ring. The sun was bright.

Mia sat as straight as she could. She spotted her parents as she turned onto the rail. Mom snapped picture after picture.

Maren stood at the center of the ring. Mia spotted Sky on Trixie. Then she saw Bobby with Erin on his back. She didn't know they were going to be here.

Mia shook her head. She couldn't worry about them. She just had to focus on showing Maren that she and Diamond had improved. That would be even better than a blue ribbon.

"Trot, riders!" Maren called out.

The horses began trotting around the ring together. Mia posted smoothly. Diamond moved at a gentle, steady pace. They trotted around the ring five times.

Then Maren lifted the white rails into place. Mia's heart sped up. This was it!

"Riders, line up for jumping!" Maren called out.

A ripple of excitement went through the riders. Mia reminded herself to stay calm and relax. "Slow and steady," she whispered.

The first horse came down the line. He hopped neatly over the rails. Then it was Sky's turn. Trixie knocked one of the rails with her foot. But they made it over. Everyone applauded.

Mia gathered up her reins. Only one more horse. Then it was her turn. She sat forward in her saddle. She reminded herself to keep her heels down. Then, out of the corner of her eye, she saw a brown blur. Bobby had spooked.

He jumped close to Diamond and knocked Diamond off-balance. The crowd gasped. Diamond whinnied. He leapt to the side. Mia saw his big neck coming up toward her.

The reins slipped from her hands. She saw the brown sand of the ring rushing toward her as she fell.

Chapter 10

# ANOTHER CHANCE

Mia sat in Maren's office. She held an ice pack to her shoulder. Sky sat next to her. Neither of them spoke. They both knew what Maren was going to say when she came in.

After Mia fell, she had gotten up and made her way from the ring. Maren had taken Diamond. She told Mia to wait in the office. Sky came for support.

They'd been waiting for fifteen minutes. But for Mia, it felt like a year. She wondered if she'd be able to visit Diamond at his new home after he was sold.

As soon as Maren walked in, she asked, "Mia, how's your shoulder?"

"Okay," Mia mumbled.

Mia thought Maren seemed awfully cheery for someone about to get rid of one of her volunteers and one of her horses.

Maren shuffled papers around on her desk. "Now, Mia," she said. "I've just been doing up the volunteer schedule for next month. I was wondering if you could increase from two days to three. We're going to be doing a spring cleaning of the stalls."

Sky and Mia looked at each other.

"Wait," Mia said. "I'm sorry, Maren, you mean Sky, right?"

Maren shook her head. "No, Mia," she said. "I mean you."

"But," Mia spluttered. "I fell off! It was a complete disaster."

"Mia, think about what happened," Maren said. "Bobby ran into Diamond. All Diamond did was try to step out of the way."

"But I lost my balance," Mia said. "I fell off my horse."

"That is nothing to be ashamed of. In fact, I was proud of you for riding so carefully. And I was proud of Diamond for not biting Bobby," Maren said.

"Me, too," Mia said.

"Yesterday I saw that you and Diamond had improved," Maren said. "I knew that if Diamond came out today wearing his bridle, then he must have learned to trust you. And you could only achieve that by being careful and slowing down."

Mia couldn't believe what she was hearing. "So, Diamond . . . ?" she asked.

"— is staying," Maren finished, grinning. "You both are."

"Yippee!" Mia couldn't help shouting. Next to her, Sky's face was plastered with a huge grin.

Mia started to leap up from her chair. She almost knocked it over. But halfway up, she stopped herself.

"Can I try that again?" she asked Maren.

As her instructor and her friend watched, Mia sat back down. Then, slowly, she rose and gave Maren a hug.

Maren laughed. "I can see you've taken this week's lessons to heart," she said.

"That's right," Mia agreed. "Maybe I should try people training next."

Maren and Sky broke into laughter.

"I think you should stick with the horses," Sky said. "Maren, can we go tell Diamond the good news?"

"Yes, go on," Maren replied, smiling. "Just —"

"— be careful!" Mia finished. "Don't worry. If I forget, Diamond will remind me."

# ABOUT THE AUTHOR

Emma Carlson Berne has written more than a dozen books for children and young adults, including teen romance novels, biographies, and history books. She lives in Cincinnati, Ohio, with her husband, Aaron, her son, Henry, and her dog, Holly.

# ABOUT THE ILLUSTRATOR

Katie Wood fell in love with drawing when she was very small. Since graduating from Loughborough University School of Art and Design in 2004, she has been living her dream working as a freelance illustrator. From her studio in Leicester, England, she creates bright and lively illustrations for books and magazines all over the world.

# GLOSSARY

**bridle** (BRYE-duhl) — straps that fit around a horse's head and mouth

**forelock** (FOR-lok) — the part of a horse's mane that falls forward between the ears

**girth** (GURTH) — the part of a horse's saddle that goes under the horse's stomach to secure the saddle

**grooming** (GROOM-ing) — brushing and cleaning a horse

**headstall** (HED-stawl) — the band that is part of a bridle that fits around a horse's head

**halters** (HAWL-turz) — straps that enclose an animal's head

**muzzle** (MUHZ-uhl) — an animal's mouth, nose, and jaw

**reins** (RAYNZ) — straps that help control a horse

**saddle** (SAD-uhl) — a seat that goes on a horse

**stable** (STAY-buhl) — a place where horses are kept

**throatlatch** (THROHT-lach) — a piece of the bridle that goes under the horse's throat

# DISCUSSION QUESTIONS

1. Sky didn't seem excited when Mia explained her new plan. Why do you think Sky responded that way? Was it right for Mia to be upset by her friend's response?

2. Mia felt confident and was riding well when Bobby got in her way. Were you surprised when Mia fell off of Diamond? Why or why not?

3. Do you think horseback riding seems difficult? Discuss your answer and reasons.

# WRITING PROMPTS

1. Mia has a problem with doing things too fast and carelessly. Write about a time when you were careless. What happened?

2. In the end, Maren gives Mia another chance. If you were Maren, would you have done the same? Write a paragraph explaining your answer.

3. Mia and Sky volunteer at the stables. Write about a place you would like to volunteer.

# HORSE FACTS

Horses swish their tails and stomp their feet on the ground when they are in pain.

When horses are angry or about to bite, they pull their ears back and show the white in their eyes.

Most horses have brown eyes. Only spotted horses, albino horses, and a few other breeds have lighter-colored eyes.

A horse's heart weighs about 10 pounds! A human heart weighs less than 1 pound.

The height of a horse is measured in hands. One hand is equal to 4 inches. The tallest horse ever recorded was Firpon. He stood 21.25 hands high and weighed 2,976 pounds.

A racehorse can lose between 15 and 25 pounds in a single race!

The average horse's stomach can hold about 5 gallons of water at one time. On a hot day, a horse can lose that much water in less than an hour!

Horses usually give birth at night. This is the time when a herd is least likely to be on the move.